I0783664

ADVERSARIES!

Dale Lazarov, TJ Wood & Captain Nikko

ADVERSARIES!

StickyGraphicNovels.com

Printed and distributed by
ComicMix, LLC.,
71 Hauxhurst Ave. Suite B
Weehawken, NJ 07086.
http://www.comicmix.com

Printed in USA.

Hardcover ISBN: 978-1-939888-63-1

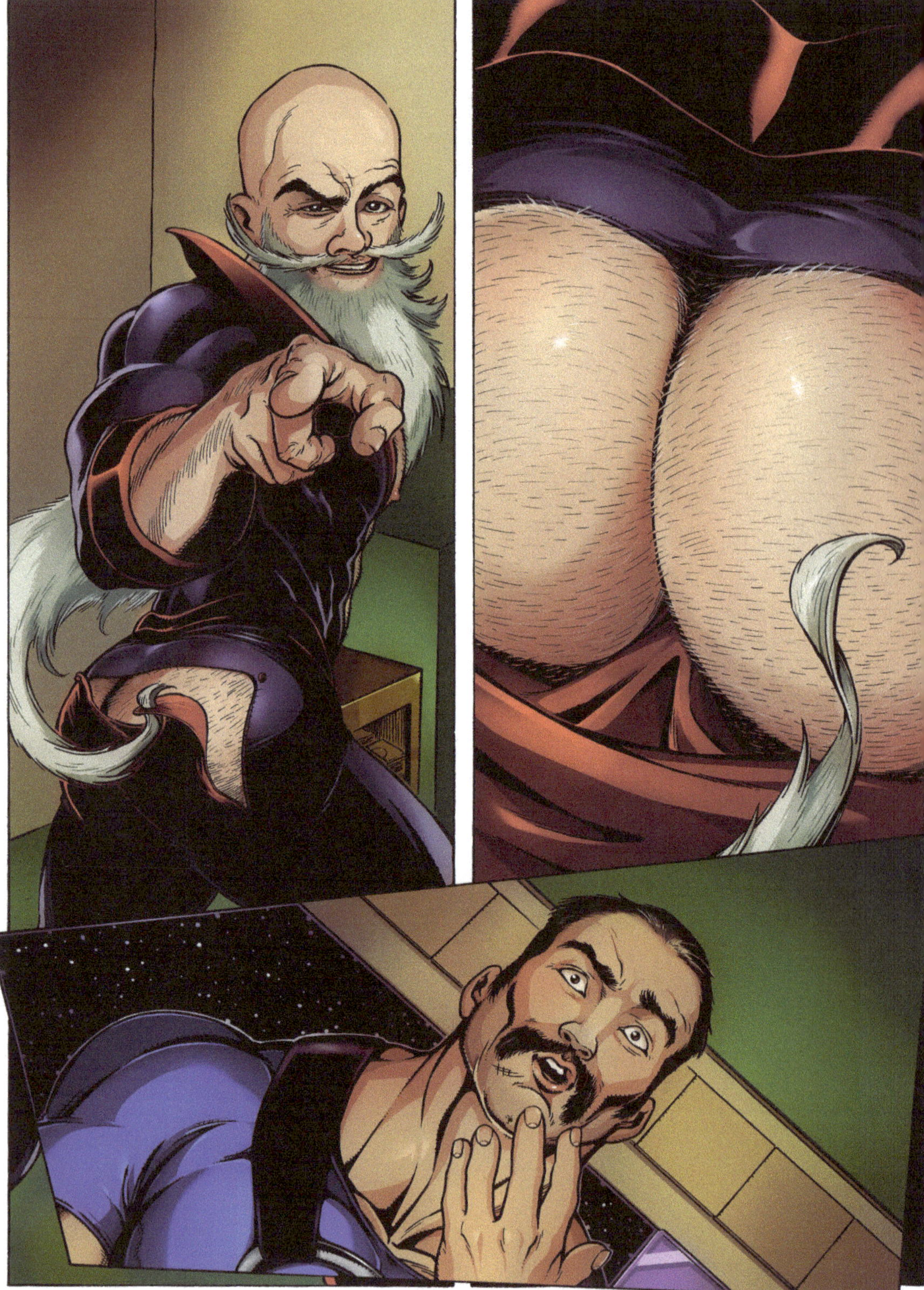

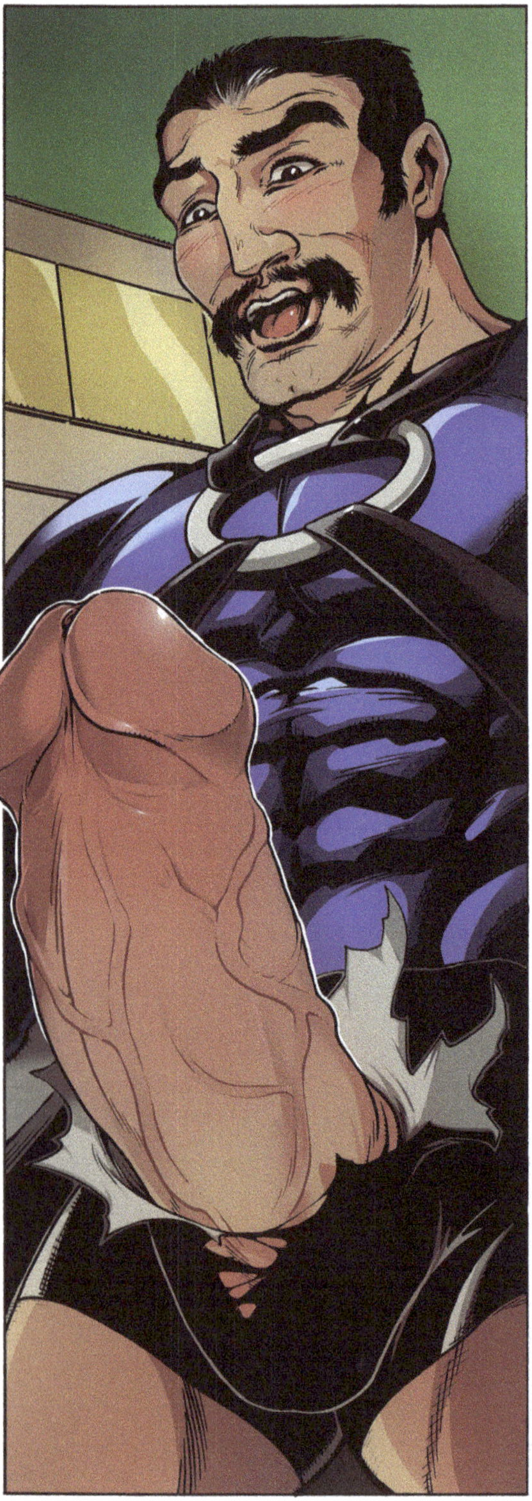

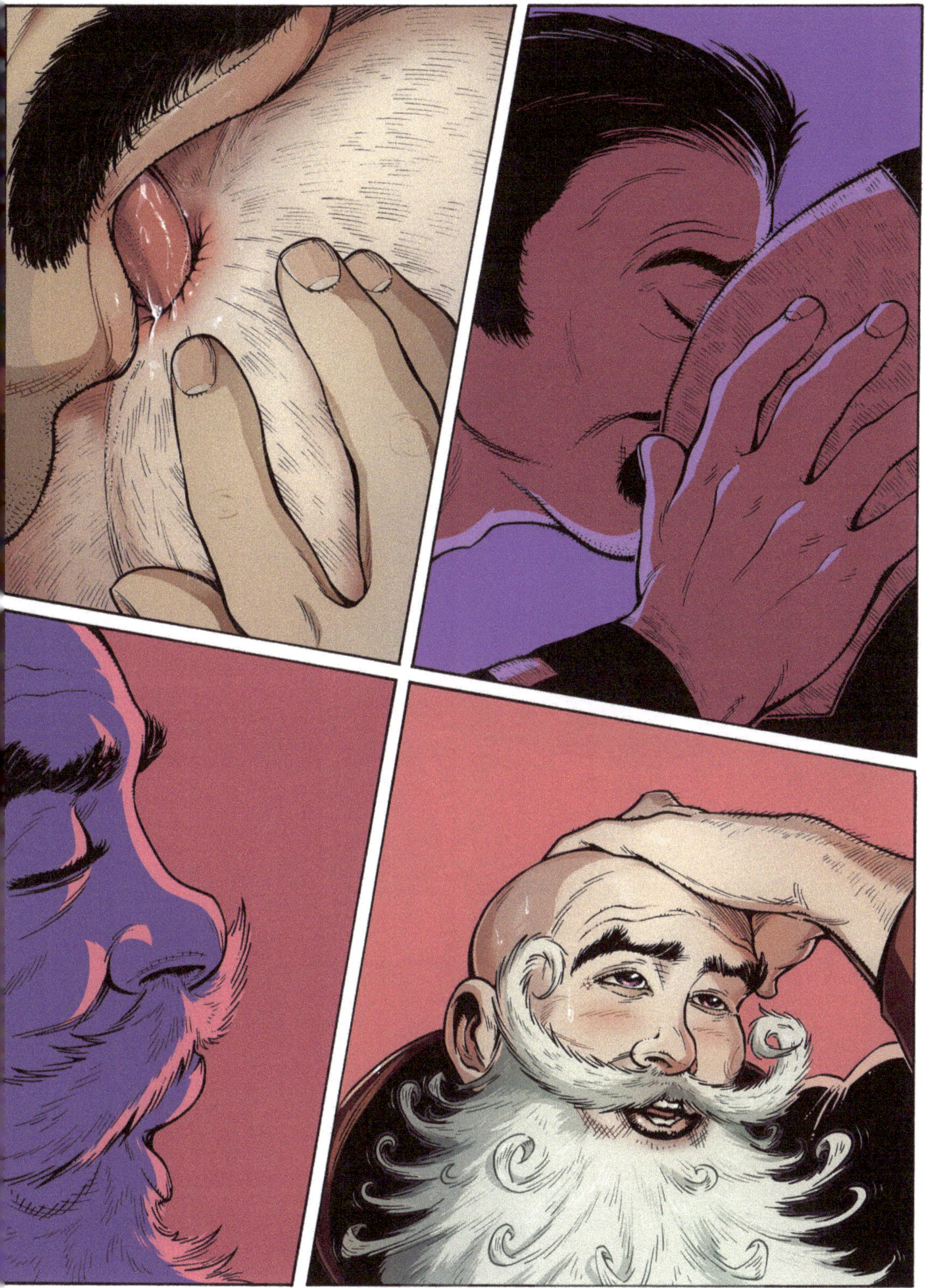

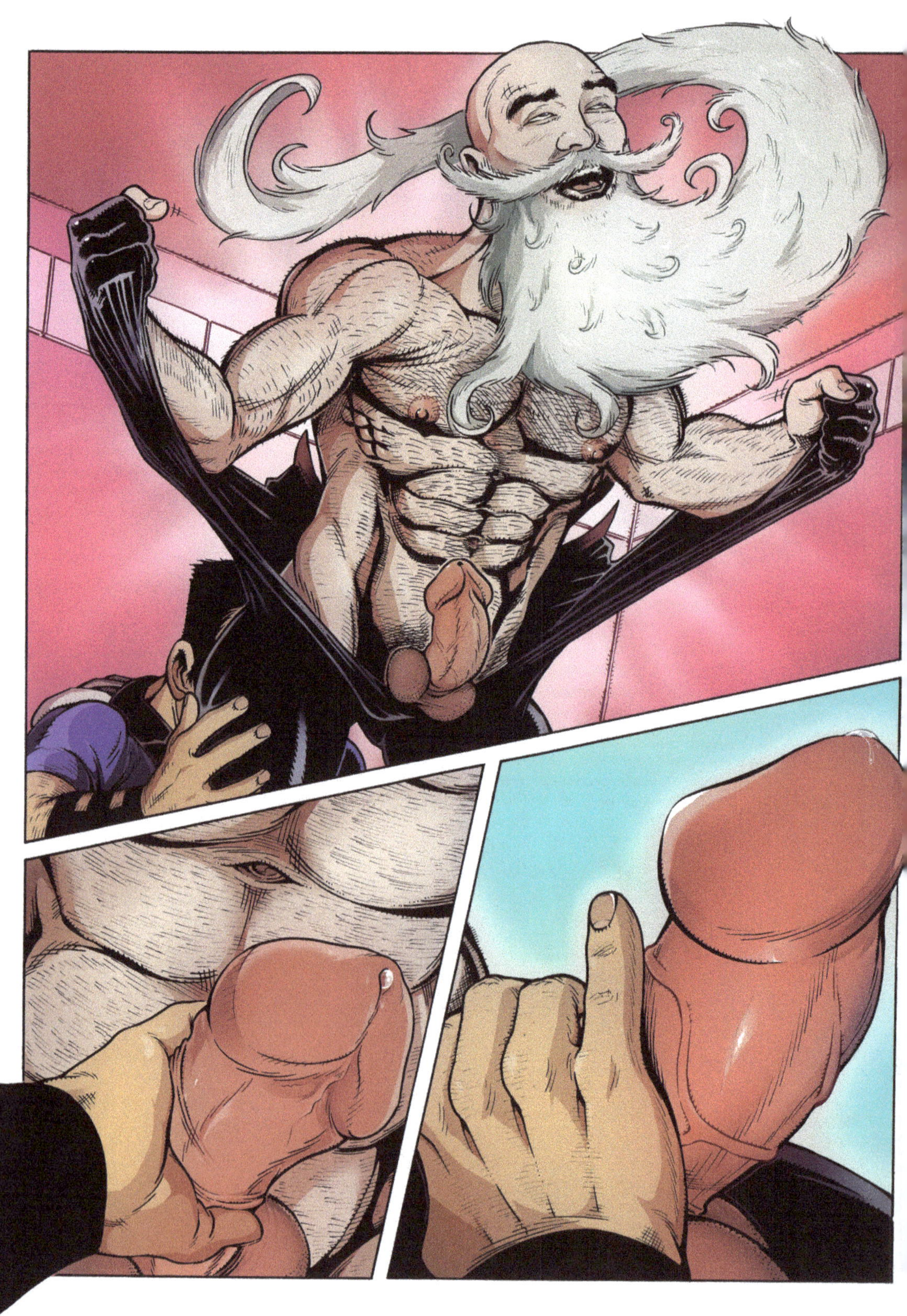

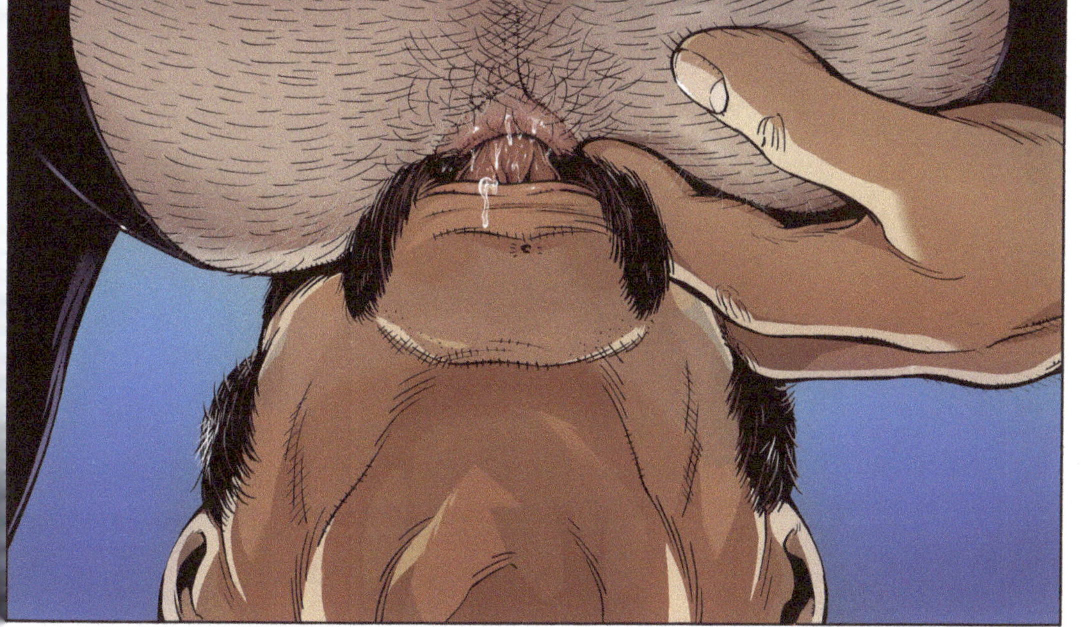

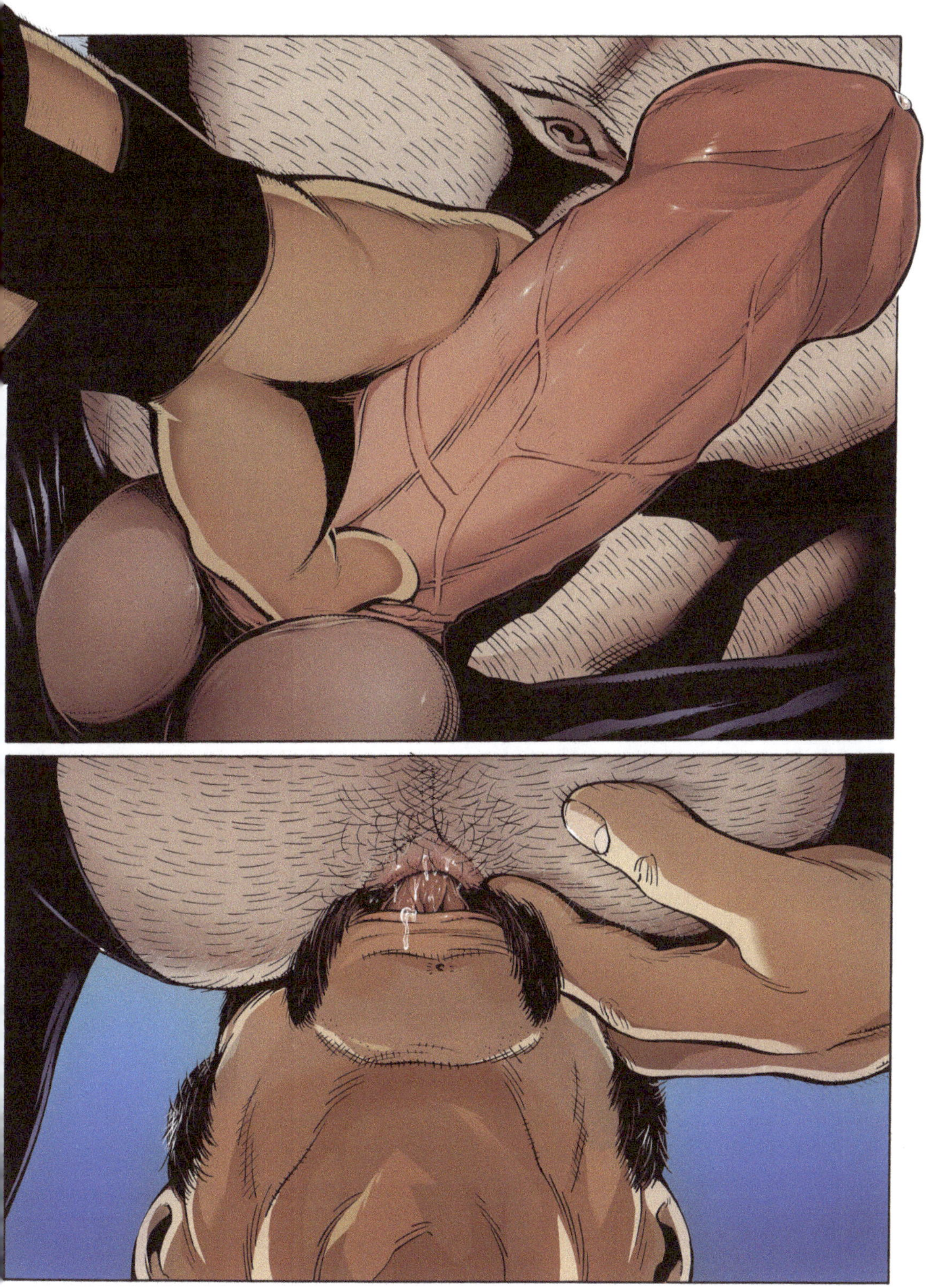

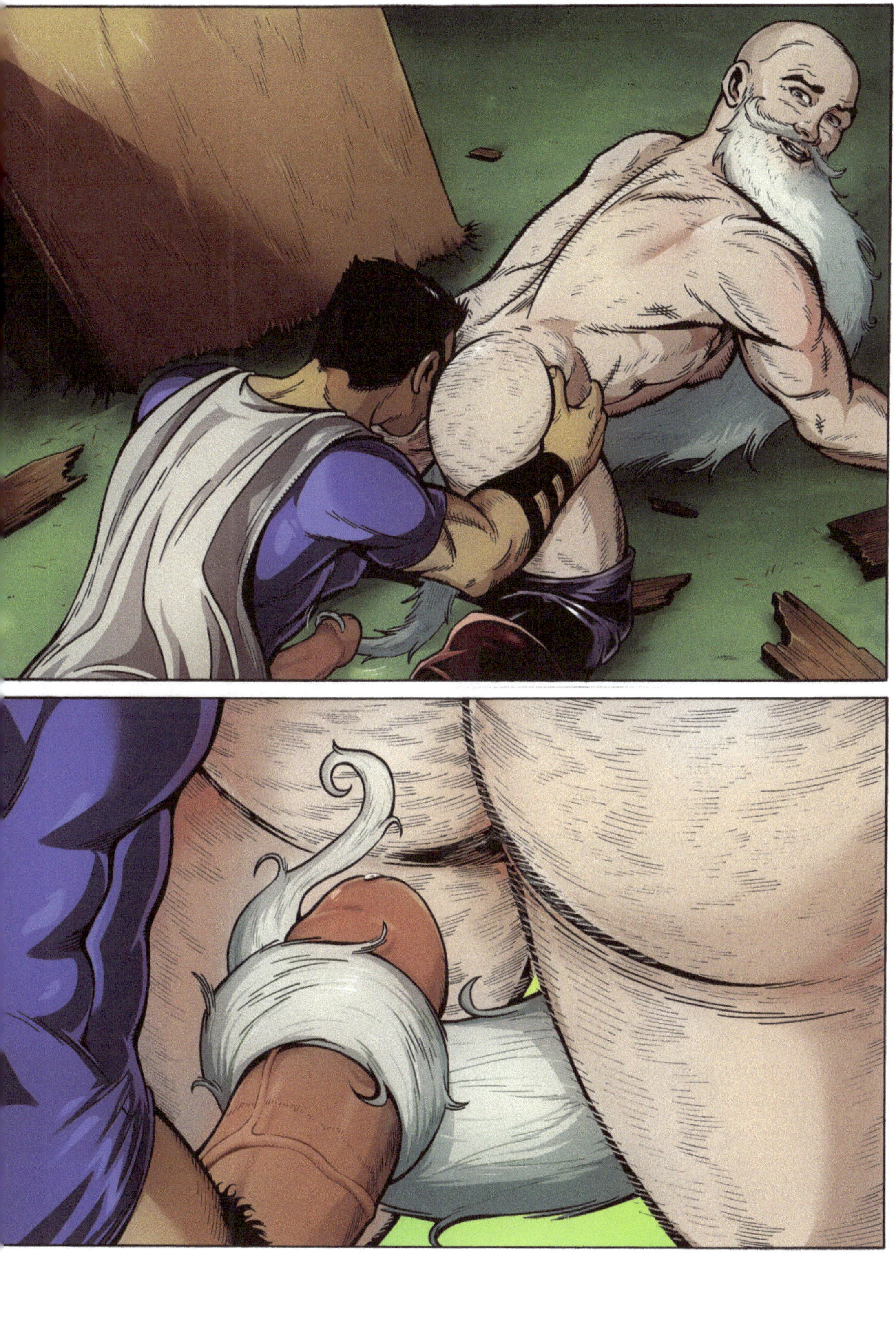

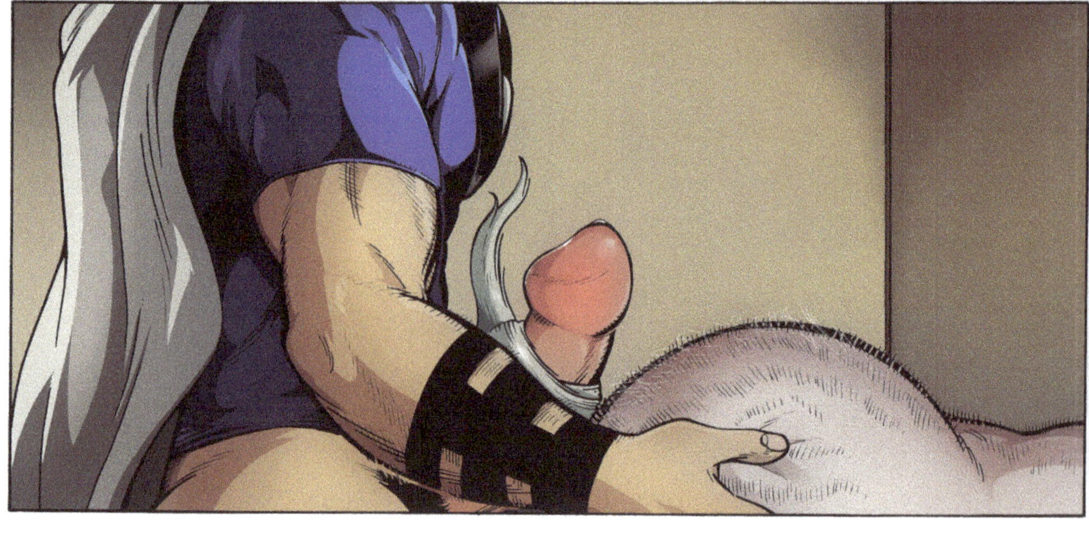

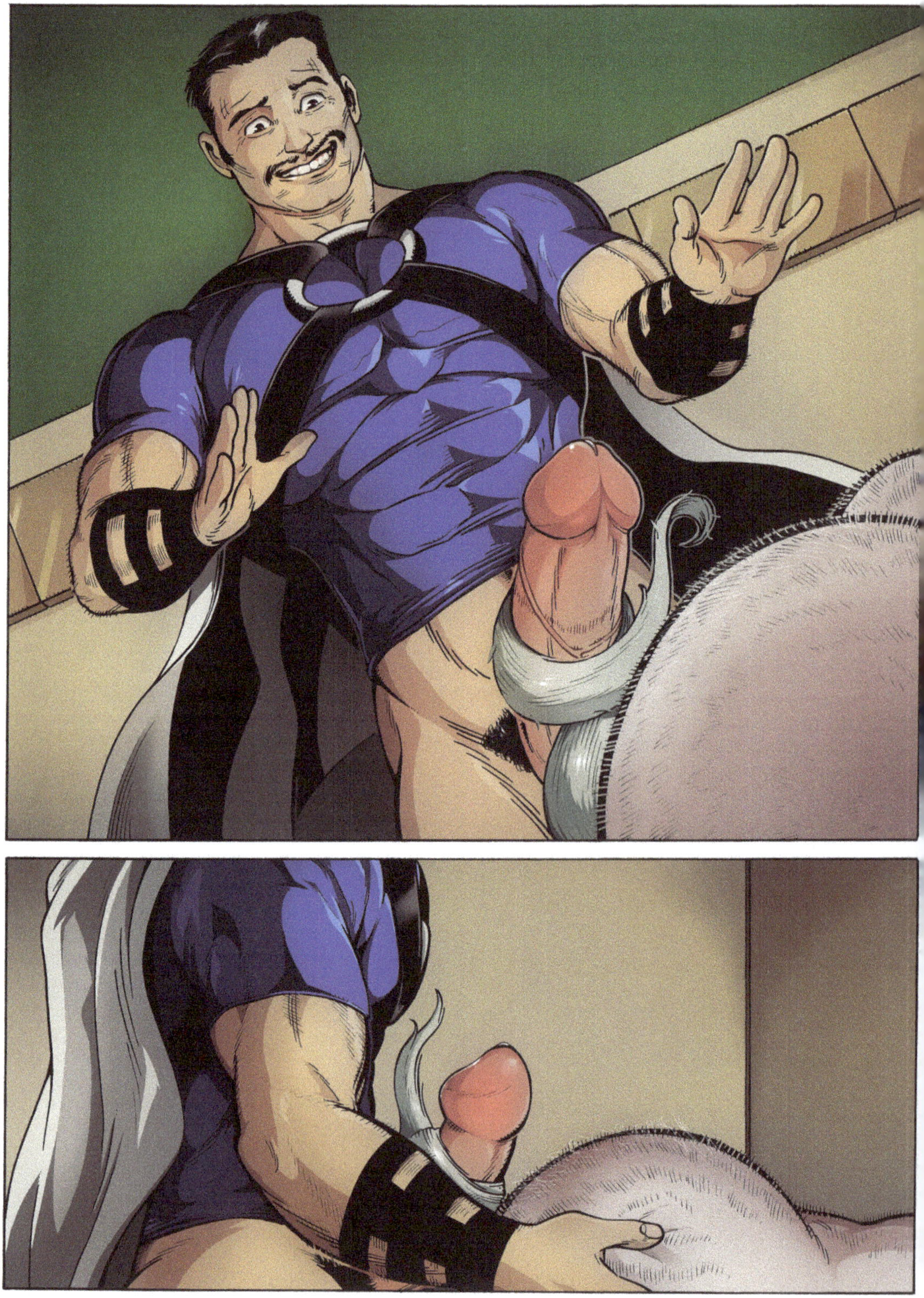

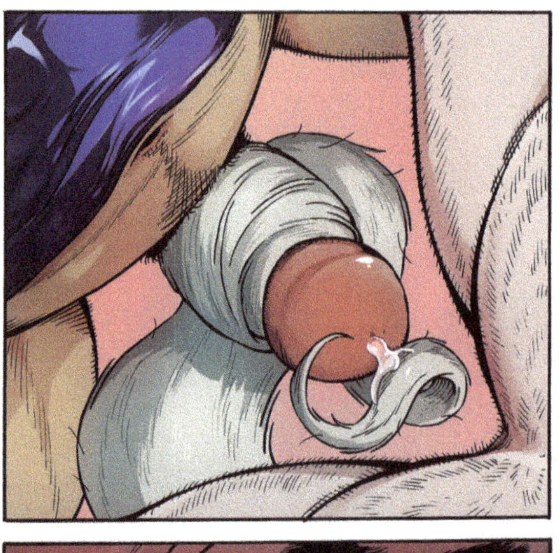
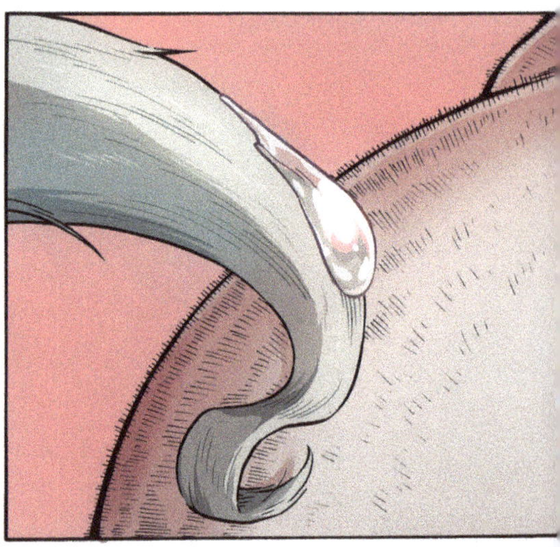
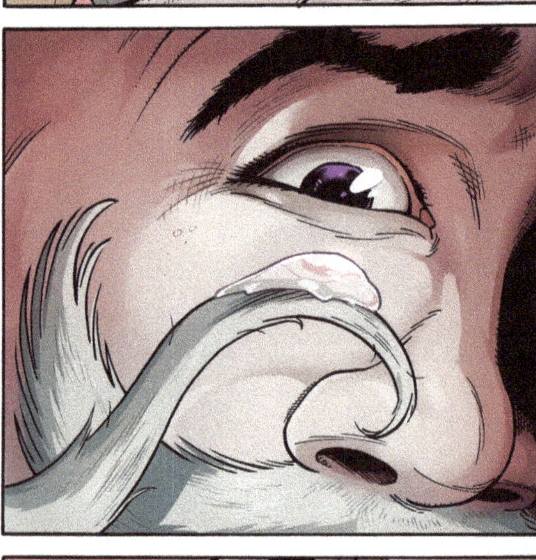

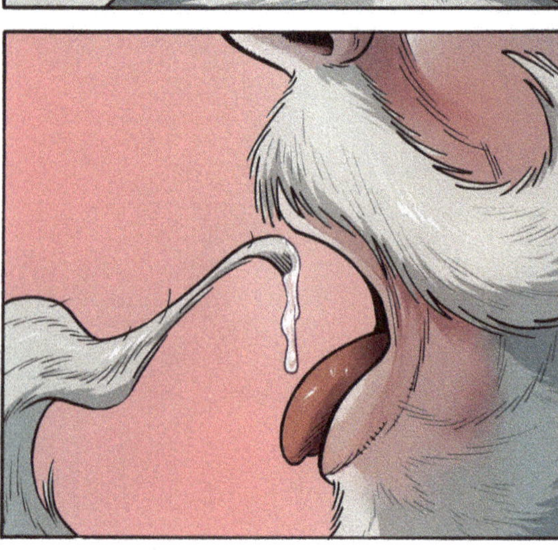
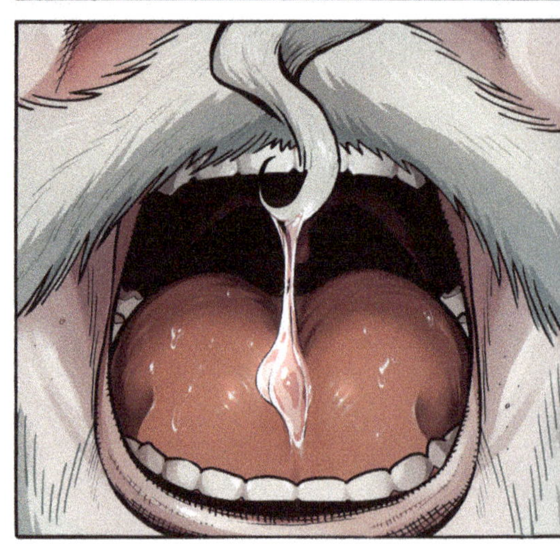

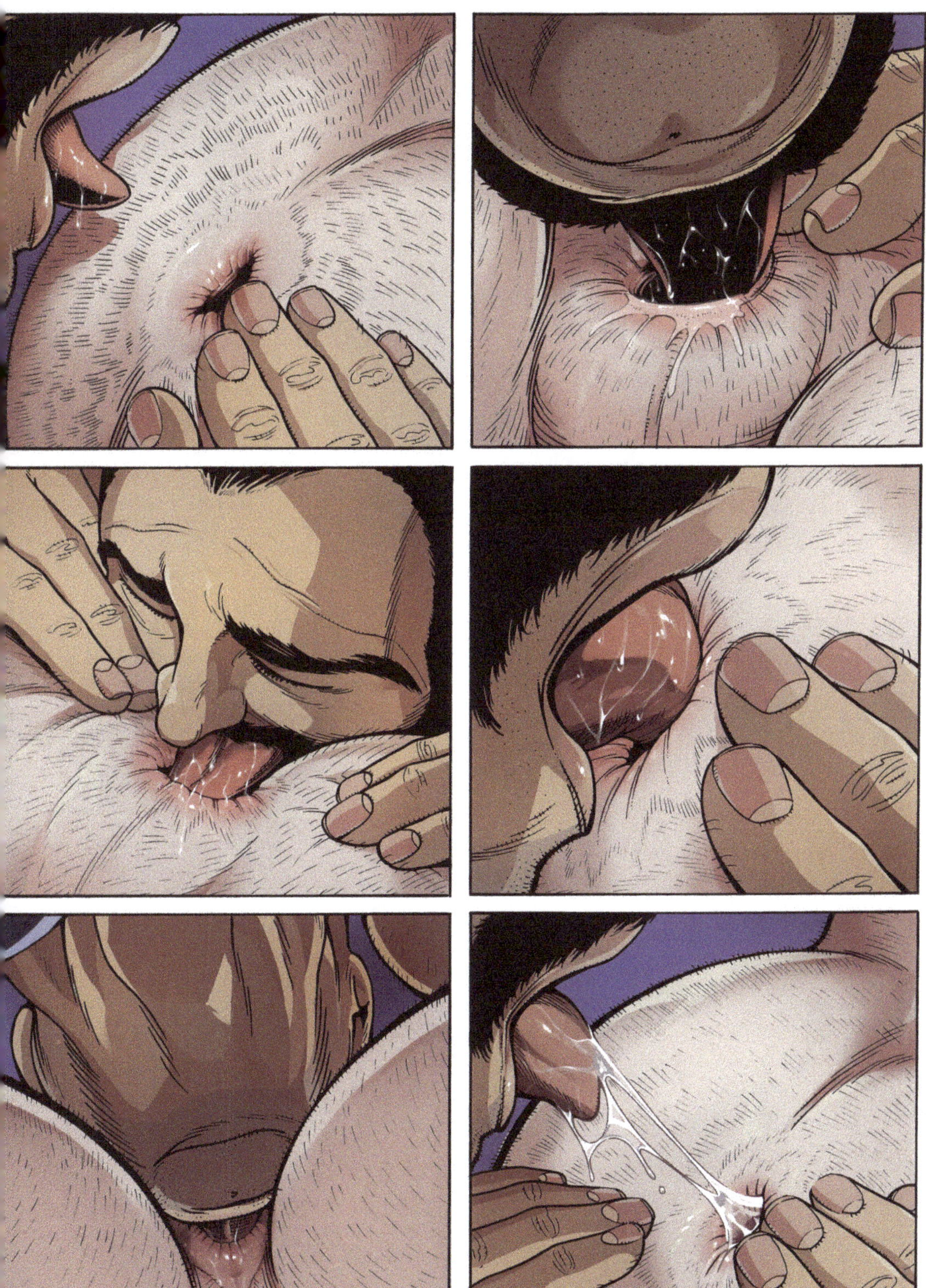

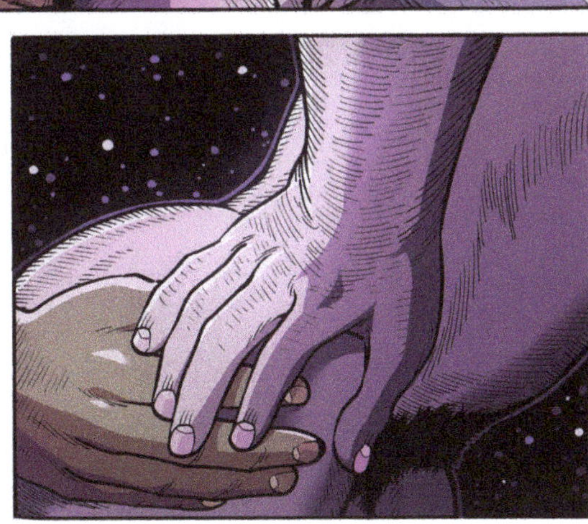

CONDEMNED FACTORY
DESIGNATED
FOR DEMOLITION

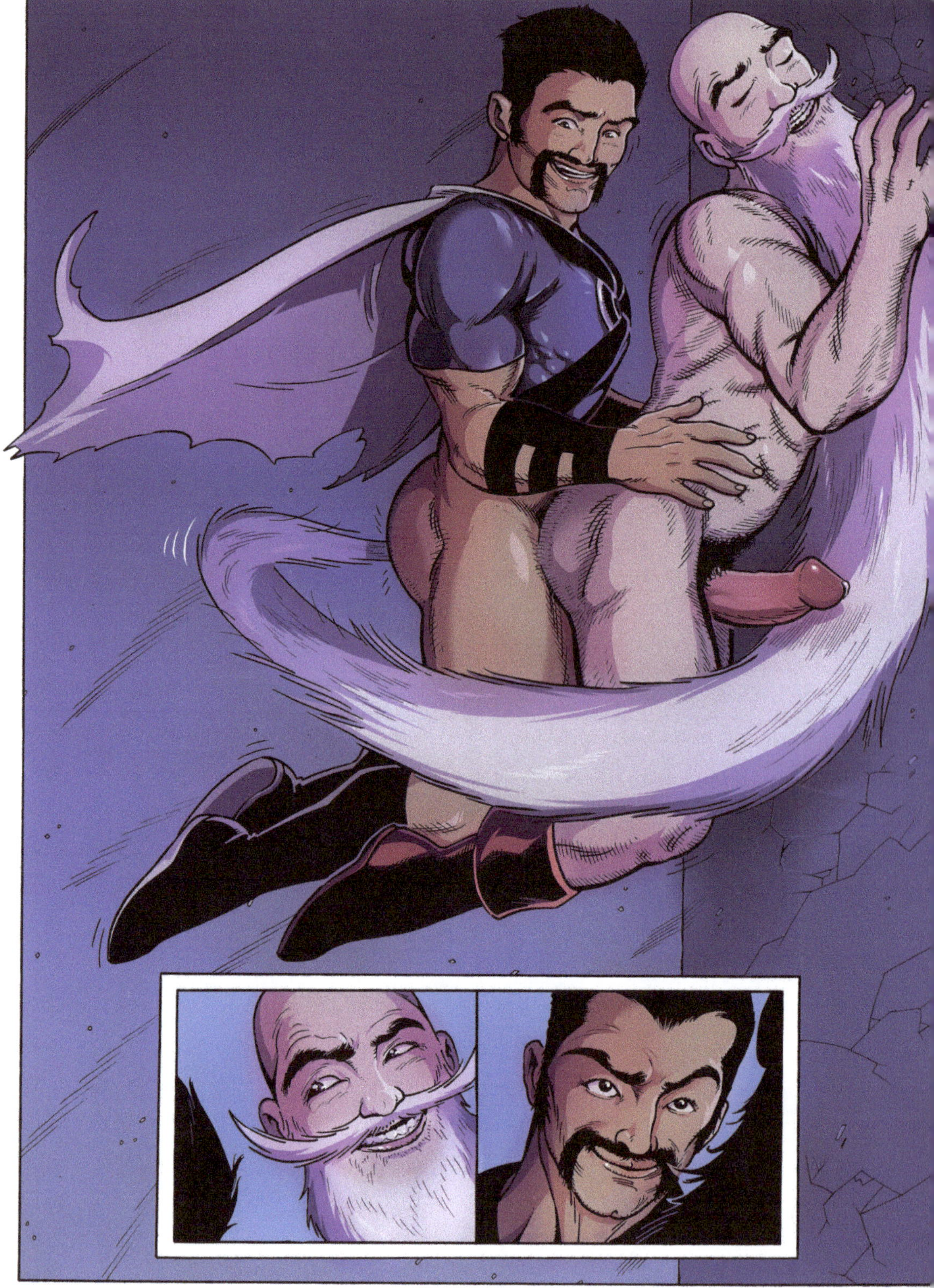

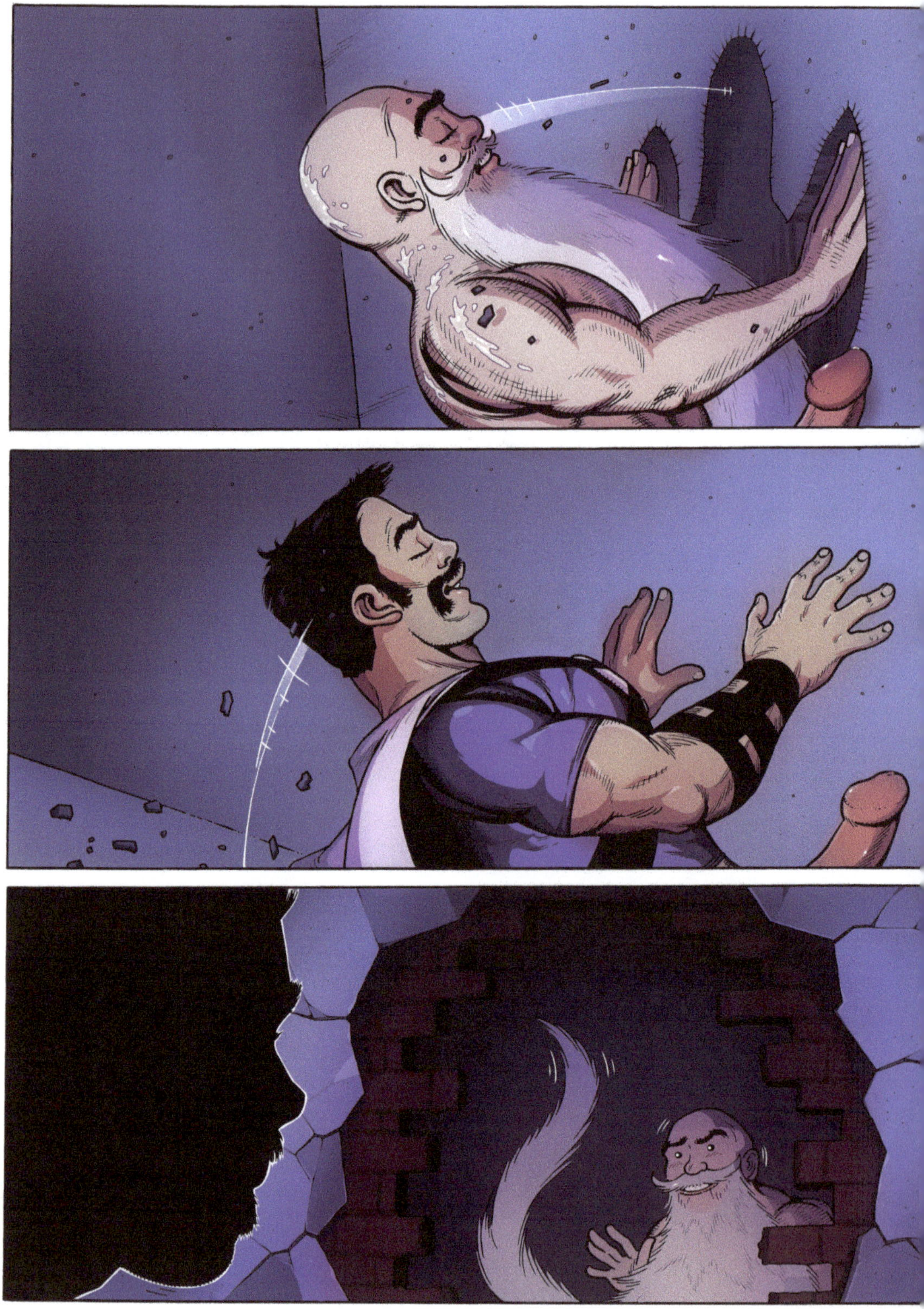

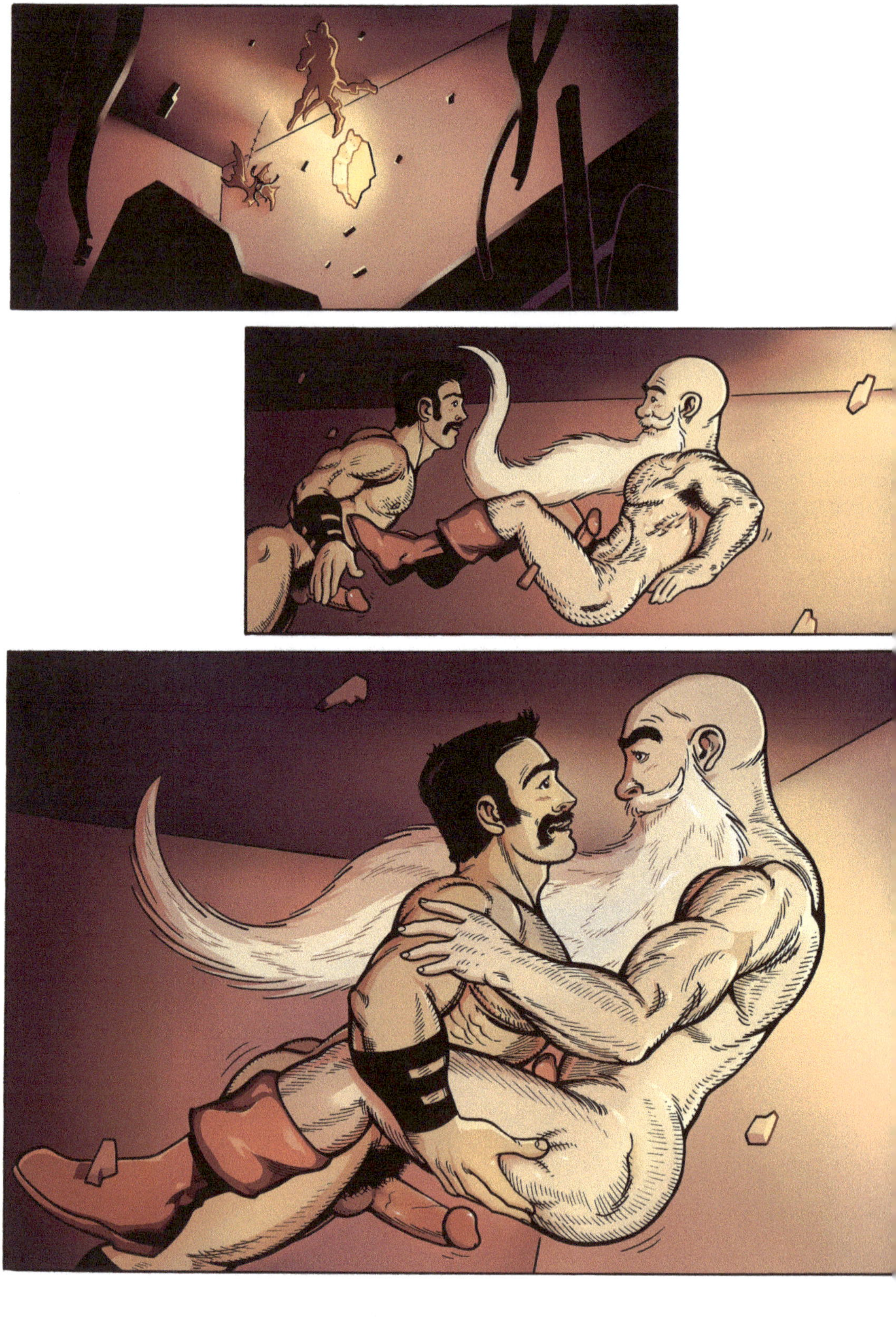

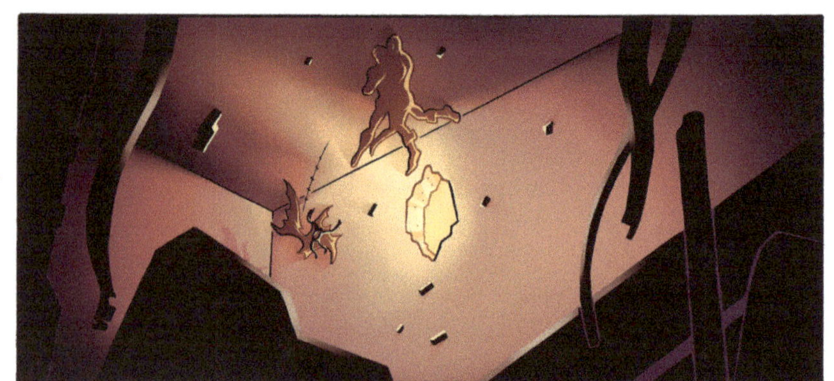

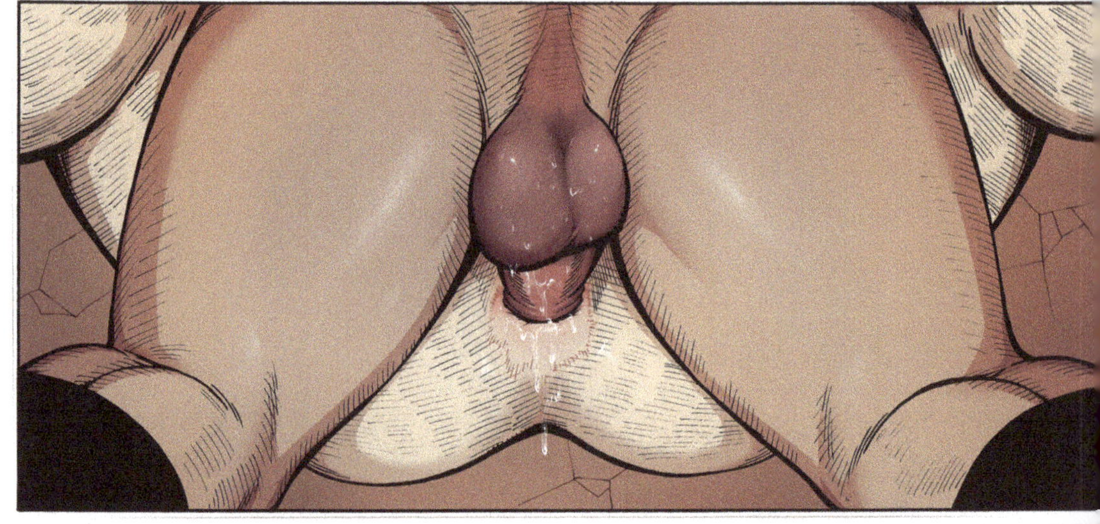

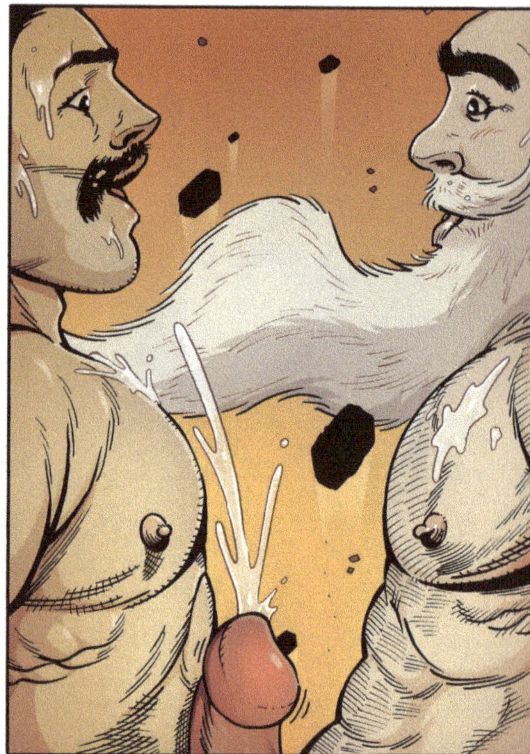

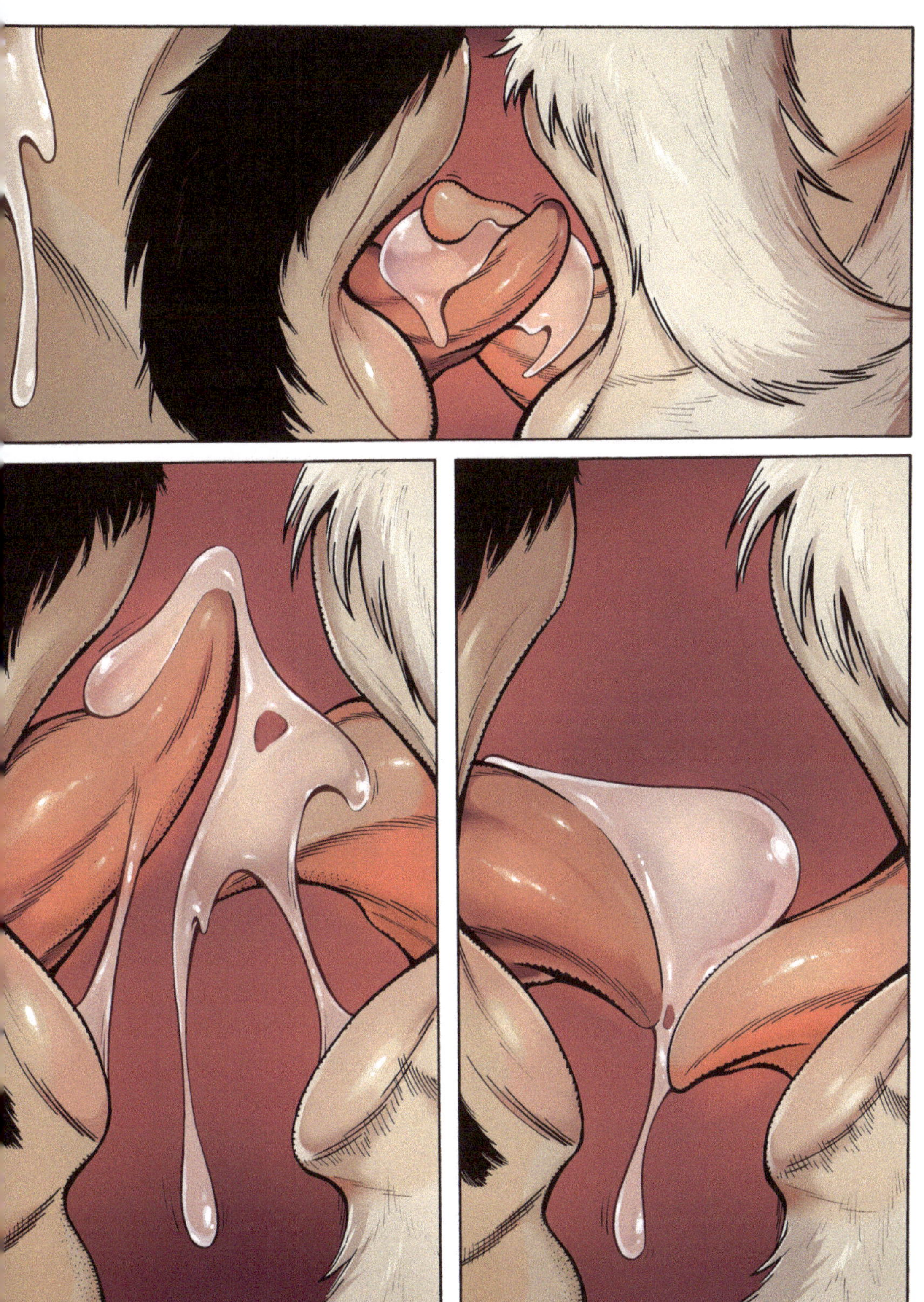

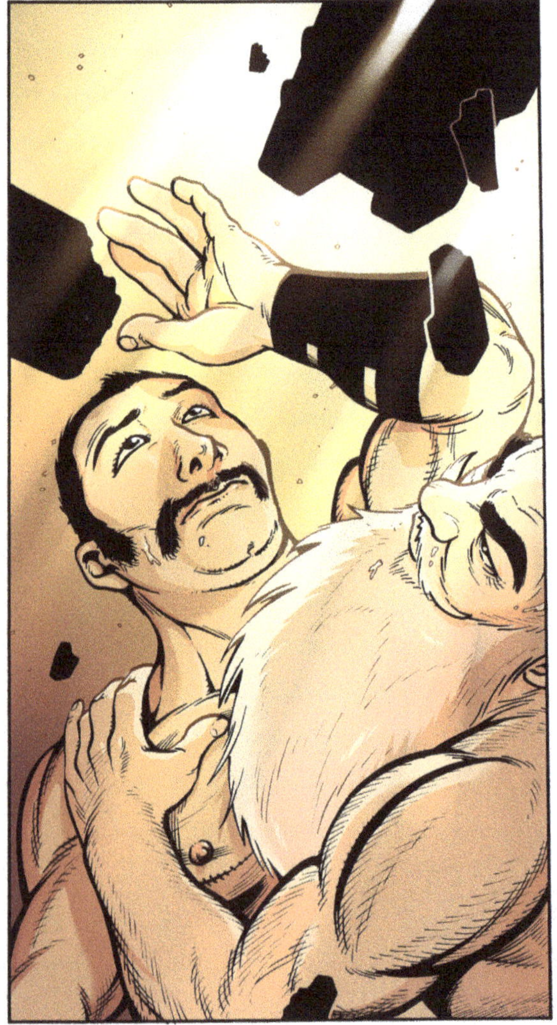

DEMOLITION INC

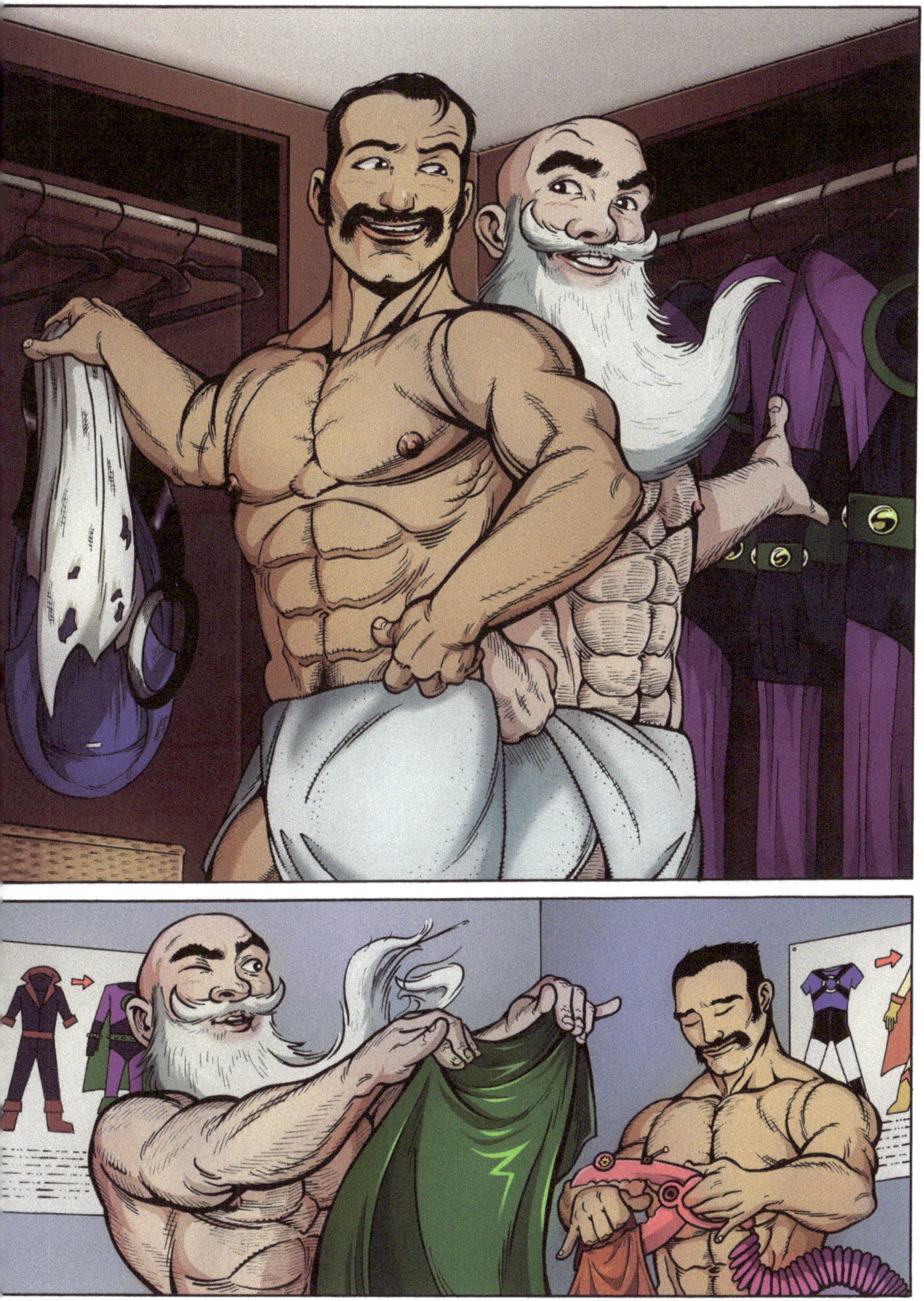

script/art direction: Dale Lazarov
linework: TJ Wood
colors: Captain Nikko

About The Authors:

Dale Lazarov is known as The Father of American Bara Comics as the writer, art director and licensor of Sticky Graphic Novels. Sticky Graphic Novels are wordless, gay character-based, sex-positive graphic novels for an international audience that are considered "a joyous expression of male/male sexuality that, while erotic, is neither grubby nor tasteless" (*The Novel Approach*). Since 2006, he has collaborated on 14 hardcover Sticky Graphic Novels and 39 digital editions with distinctive and evocative gay comics artists from around the globe. In his secret identity, he is Aldo Alvarez, Ph.D., and lives in Chicago.

TJ Wood has produced gay erotic art for over twenty years, including the *Crash Course* series (Class Comics) with writer Johnny Murdoc, numerous short stories and many commissioned pieces. He holds a Bachelor's degree in Art and Art History from Exeter University - in his native UK - and cites key influences from Michelangelo to Tom of Finland and Zack. Comic books have been his long-standing passion - particularly those from Marvel and DC. Through his Deviant Art webpage at https://tjwood-uk.deviantart.com/, TJ creates commissioned artwork for his many devotees and administrates a fetish art group.

Captain Nikko is a New York born artist working primarily in the online gay erotica and anthro communities. Living in Manhattan he posts his artwork and comics on his Furaffinity (http://www.furaffinity.net/user/captainnikko/), Tumblr (https://nikkonator5000.tumblr.com/) and his Patreon (https://www.patreon.com/Nikkonator) where he shares both his original comics and collaborative works. ADVERSARIES is his first published project.

www.ingramcontent.com/pod-product-compliance
Lightning Source LLC
Chambersburg PA
CBHW051119300726
48981CB00002B/189